George
_____

With love from
Jenny and Murdoch.
Christmas 1988

*Railway Series, No. 24*

# OLIVER THE WESTERN ENGINE

by
### THE REV. W. AWDRY

with illustrations by
GUNVÖR & PETER EDWARDS

HEINEMANN · LONDON

William Heinemann Ltd
Michelin House
81 Fulham Road
London SW3 6RB

LONDON   MELBOURNE   AUCKLAND

First published by Kaye & Ward Ltd
Copyright © 1969 William Heinemann Ltd
Reprinted 1988

ISBN 0 434 92801 1

Printed and bound in Great Britain by
William Clowes Limited, Beccles and London

# FOREWORD

Dear M.,

We both wanted to call this book Little Western Engines; but Publishers are stern men. They did not approve.

They, of course, don't know the trouble we've had with Oliver. We hope he has learnt sense, but goodness knows what will happen when he finds he has a book all to himself . . . .

I know! If Oliver gets uppish, we'll set Messrs. Kaye & Ward on to him. That'll teach him!                                    W.

READERS may like to know that "Olivers" and "Ducks" still work on the Dart Valley Railway in Devonshire; and "Small Railway Engines" are at Ravenglass in Cumberland.

# Donald's Duck

THE Fat Controller has re-opened a Branch Line. It runs along the coast by sandy beaches and seaside towns till it meets the Small Railway at a port to which big ships come.

As Duck had made friends with the Small Railway Engines, the Fat Controller asked him to take charge. "Your work in the Yard has been good," he said kindly. "Would you like to have this Branch Line for your own?"

"Yes, please, Sir," said Duck.

"Very well," said the Fat Controller. "I hope you will work hard, and be a credit to me."

Duck is very proud of his Branch Line, and he works very hard. His two coaches, Alice and Mirabel, are painted in Great Western colours. They take passengers to the Small Railway.

Duck also has some trucks in which he hauls away the ballast that the Small Engines bring down from their valley. The Fat Controller uses this ballast for his railway.

Duck cannot do all the work himself, so Donald and Douglas take turns to help him. The Fat Controller has built them a shed at the station by the Small Railway.

Duck felt his responsibility deeply. He talked endlessly about it.

"You don't understand, Donald, how much the Fat Controller relies on me."

"Och aye", muttered Donald sleepily.

"I'm Great Western and . . . ."

"Quack, quack, quack."

"What?"

"Ye heard. Quack, quack ye go, syne ye'd an egg laid. Now wheesht, and let an engine sleep."

"Quack yourself," said Duck indignantly. He stayed awake wondering how to pay Donald out. At last he said to himself sleepily, "I'll ask Driver in the morning."

"He says I quack as if I'd laid an egg.
Let's pay him out."

"Quack, do you?" His Fireman pondered.
"I know," he said, and whispered.

Duck giggled, and his Driver slapped his
leg in delight. "Just right," he said. He dearly
loved a joke.

That night, when Donald was asleep, they
popped something into his water tank. "We've
done it!" they whispered to Duck

"They won't hurt her, will they?" asked
Duck anxiously.

"Bless you, no. They're both kind men.
She'll come to no harm."

A duckling popped out of Donald's tank at the first water-stop. Both Driver and Fireman goggled with surprise, but Donald laughed.

"Na doot at a' who's behind this," he said, and told them what had happened in the shed.

The duckling was tame. She shared the Driver's and Fireman's sandwiches, and rode in the tender, quacking at intervals. The other engines enjoyed teasing Donald about her.

Presently, however, she hopped off at a station, and, as they couldn't wait to catch her – there she stayed.

But before they reached home, Donald, and his Driver and Fireman, consulted together, and made a plan.

That night, Donald's Driver and Fireman got busy.

When Duck's crew arrived to look him over in the morning, they found something which made them laugh till they cried.

"Look, Duck!" they said. "Look what was under your bunker – a nest-box with an egg in it!"

Duck peered at it unbelievingly.

Donald opened a sleepy eye. "Ye dinna say!" he exclaimed. "D'ye mind what I said, Duck? Ye must ha' laid it this night, all unbeknownst!"

Then Duck laughed too. "You win, Donald," he said. "It'd take a clever engine to get the better of you!"

The duckling settled at the station, and became a pet with passengers and staff.

She carefully inspects all parcels and luggage, and sees that the porters stow them properly in the vans.

When she wants a swim, she flies to a nearby pond, but always returns to welcome the trains. She stands by the cab, quacking imperiously, till driver or fireman gives her something to eat.

Donald is her favourite, and she sometimes allows him to give her rides, but always gets off at her own station.

The Stationmaster calls her Dilly, but to everyone else, she is always Donald's Duck.

## Resource and Sagacity

OLIVER is a Great Western tank engine. The Other Railway wanted to scrap him, so he ran away. Isabel, his faithful coach, came too, and so did Toad, a brake van.

At the last moment they were nearly caught, but Douglas saved them. The Fat Controller was pleased, and said that when Oliver was mended he could help Duck with his Branch Line.

"We'll give you Great Western colours, like Duck," he said kindly. "That will help you to forget your troubles."

"Oh, thank you, Sir," said Oliver happily.

Duck's Branch starts from the Big Station. When Oliver started work, he often met other engines there. They all wanted to know about his adventures.

"Amazing!" Henry would remark.

"Oliver," said James, "has resource . . . ."

" . . . and sagacity," put in Gordon. "He is an example to us all."

"You're *too* kind," giggled Oliver modestly. But he was only a tank engine after all. No big engine had ever said admiring things to him before. I'm sorry to say that it made him puffed up in the smokebox.

The Fat Controller rescued another coach, called Dulcie. She trundled along with Isabel.

Oliver sang "Oh, Isabel's a funny coach and so is Dulcie too. If I didn't look after them, they'd not know what to do!"

"Just listen to him. Just *listen* to him," twittered Dulcie.

"He's proud, he's conceited; he's heading for trouble," Isabel sadly replied. "I feel it in my *frames*," she shrieked as they rounded a curve.

Oliver just laughed. "Henry says I'm amazing. He's right. What do I care for trouble. I just push it aside."

All trucks are badly behaved, but ballast trucks are worst of all. Donald, Douglas, and Duck warned Oliver about this.

"You think I can't manage," he said huffily. "Gordon knows better. *He* says I'm sagacious."

"You may be 'goodgracious', but ... ."

"Say no more, Duck. It's mebbe a peety, but the wee engine'll juist ha ta learrn."

Today, Oliver took the trucks by himself for the first time. He pulled the loaded ones to a siding and pushed "empties" to the Chute. Then he came back full of confidence to take the loaded wagons away.

The loaded trucks were comfortable, and didn't want to move. They had just realised, too, that they had a different engine. "Duck, we know," they grumbled, "and Donald, and Douglas. What right has Oliver to poke his funnel in here?"

"Look sharp!" puffed Oliver. "Smartly there!"

"That's not the way to speak! Pay him out!" The trucks moved off easily, and Oliver thought he had them in control.

"Trucks," he told himself proudly, "daren't play tricks on ME! I'll arrange them on the middle road, and start away as soon as Duck arrives. I can't understand why he says they're so troublesome."

They reached the station throat. Oliver's brakes came on with a groan. But brakes were useless against loaded surging trucks. They pushed forward yelling, "ON! ON! ON!"

Oliver fought hard, but still they forced him on, and on, and on.

Their effort slackened at last. "I'm winning," he gasped. "If only . . . ."

But it was too late. One moment his rear wheels were on the rails; the next, they had none, and he was bunker down in the turntable well, with a deluge of ballast all round him.

When Duck arrived, he was stopped outside the Station, and flagged to the platform.

He surveyed the wreckage. "Hullo Oliver!" he remarked, "Are you being a 'goodgracious' engine? Beg pardon, of course, but we don't *really* like that sort of surprise. Donald and Douglas will miss their turntable."

Later that day, Donald and Douglas spoke pungently in Scots, and the Fat Controller spoke pointedly in English. All three left Oliver in no doubt at all, that so far from being sagacious, he was a very silly engine.

## Toad stands by

WHEN Oliver came home again, the trucks sang rude songs. They were led by Scruffey, a "Private Owner" wagon.

"Oliver's no use at all; thinks he's very clever.
Says that he can manage us; that's the best joke ever!
When he orders us about, with the greatest folly,
We just push him down the well. Pop – goes old Ollie!"

The engines bumped them. "Shut up!" they ordered. But they couldn't be everywhere; and everywhere they weren't, the trucks began again.

At last they gave it up. "We're sorry, Oliver," they said.

"It's really my fault," he answered sadly.

"I'm worried, Mr Douglas," said Toad next morning. "This nasty spirit of disrespect for engines. Where's it going to end?"

"Dear knaws," said Douglas gloomily.

"It must be stopped before it gets worse. I believe Mr Oliver can do it."

"Mebbe so, but how?"

"I've a plan, Mr Douglas. May I stay here today and help him? We are both Great Western and must stand together. Would you ask him, before you go, to favour me with a word?"

"I'll take ye to him; but he's ower sma' for the wurrk ye ha in mind."

"  . . . No, Duck, Toad's right. This trouble's my fault, and I must put it right."

"I meant no disrespect, you understand."

"Of course not, Toad. Anyway, Driver says the same, and he's arranged it with Station-master."

"Very well, Oliver; but I must hurry. My passengers'll be waiting. Don't forget Stepney's tip about sand. Lay it on the rails as you back down, and roll it firm with your wheels. You get a splendid grip that way. Good luck! We three'll be there to cheer you on while you give those trucks a lesson."

"So long!" smiled Oliver bravely: but he felt dreadfully nervous inside.

"I expect, Mr Oliver, you'll want me on the middle road as a stop-block, like."

"Er – Yes, please."

Oliver marshalled the worst trucks two by two in front of Toad.

"This way, Mr Oliver, takes longer, but they can't give trouble, and if you leave that Scruffey till last, you'll have him behind you. Then you can bump him if he starts his nonsense."

Duck arrived to find them ready and waiting.

"Three cheers for Oliver and Toad!" he called. Alice and Mirabel responded with a will, and so, wonderingly, did the passengers.

"Hold back!" whispered Scruffey. The trucks giggled as they passed the word.

Oliver dug his wheels into the sand, and gave a mighty heave.

"Ooer!" groaned Scruffey. His couplings tightened. He was stretched between Oliver and the trucks. "I don't like this!"

"Go it!" yelled Duck. "Well done, Boy, WELL DONE!"

"OW! OW!" wailed Scruffey, but no-one bothered about him. "OW! OOOOOW! I'm coming apaaaaaart!"

There came a rending, splitting crash.

Oliver shot forward suddenly. Scruffey's front end bumped behind his bunker, while Scruffey's load spread itself over the track.

"Well, Oliver, so you don't know your own strength! Is that it?"

"N-n-no, Sir," said Oliver nervously.

The Fat Controller inspected the remains.

"As I thought," he remarked. "Rotten wood, rusty frames – unserviceable before it came." He winked at Oliver, and whispered, "Don't tell the trucks that – bad for discipline!"

He strode away, chuckling.

Nowadays, Oliver only takes trucks when the other engines are busy; but they always behave well. "Take care with Mr Oliver," they warn each other. "He's strong he is. You play tricks on him, and he'll likely pull you in half."

# Bulgy

It was Bank Holiday morning. The Small Railway Engines were working hard. Their station was crowded. No sooner had one train started than another was filled with people waiting to go.

Duck, Oliver, Donald, and Douglas were busy too; but they had not brought everybody. The Yard was full of parked cars and coaches.

Duck was waiting for his next turn. Alice and Mirabel complained of the heat, so he backed them into the Goods Shed while he basked outside in the sun.

Near him stood a huge red bus. He had never seen it before.

The bus watched the passengers happily "milling" round the Small Railway.

"Stupid nonsense!" he grumbled. "Wouldn't have brought 'em if I'd known. I'd have had a breakdown or something."

"I'm glad you didn't," smiled Duck. "You'd have spoilt their fun. Look how they're enjoying themselves!"

"Pah!" snorted the bus. "Enjoyment's all you engines live for, taking the petrol from the tanks of us workers. Come the Revolution," he went on fiercely, "railways'll be ripped up. Cars 'nd coaches 'll trample their remains."

"Free the roads," he growled. "Free the roads from Railway Tyranny!"

At the passing station Duck told Oliver about the bus. "I call him 'Bulgy'," he chuckled. "He's painted bright red and shouts 'Down with railways'."

But next time they met, Oliver didn't laugh.

"Bulgy's friend has come," he said. "He's red and rude too. He's taking Bulgy's passengers home, so's to leave him free to steal ours."

"But he can't," objected Duck. "Ours want to go to the Big Station."

"Bulgy bets he can get there before us."

"Rubbish! It's much further by road."

Oliver looked anxious. "Yes, but Bulgy says he knows a short cut."

That evening Donald, Oliver, and Duck were preparing for the homeward rush. Duck's train was to be first out, but he had few passengers. He was soon to know why!

"Look!" shrilled Oliver. "Look at Bulgy! He's a mean Scarlet Deceiver!"

Bulgy had turned to leave. They could now see his other side. It had on it RAILWAY BUS.

"STOP!" yelled Staff and engines, but too late.

"Yah! Booh! Snubs!" jeered Bulgy. He roared away. The unsuspecting passengers waved happily.

"Come on!" puffed Duck. He, Alice and Mirabel trundled unhappily away.

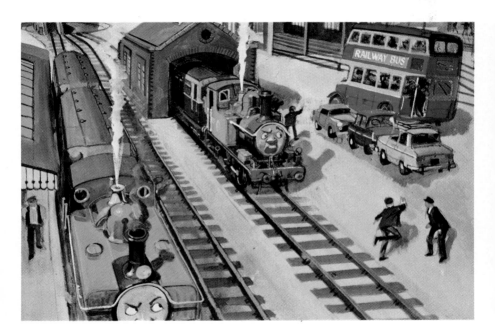

Alice and Mirabel chattered crossly. "The nasty old thief, he's stolen our people!"

Duck wondered how to pay Bulgy out.

Then, far ahead, a man clambered up the embankment waving a red scarf. "Danger!" he shouted.

The line here crosses a narrow road. Duck came as close as he could. "So *this* was Bulgy's short cut!" He chuckled.

Bulgy was wedged under the bridge. Drivers of cars trapped in front and behind were telling him what they thought. Angry passengers, cornering the Conductor, demanded their money back.

From time to time loosened bricks fell making Bulgy yelp.

Bulgy's passengers swarmed round Duck.

"He tricked us," they complained. "He said he was a railway bus, but wouldn't accept our return tickets. He wanted us to think railways are no good. Please help us."

Duck's crew examined the bridge. "It's risky," they said, "but we must help the passengers."

"Passengers are 'Urgent'," agreed Duck. "Besides," he chuckled, "it'll pay Bulgy out!"

They laughed, and told the passengers to wait on the other side of the bridge.

"STOP!" wailed Bulgy. "It might *fall* on me!"

"That," said Duck severely, "would serve you right for telling 'whoppers'."

Bulgy howled as he felt the bridge quiver, but it didn't collapse. Duck made good time to the Big Station, and all passengers caught their trains.

The Fat Controller arranged a "shuttle service" on the Branch. Passengers changed trains at Bulgy's Bridge.

Bulgy had to stay till it was mended, but he never learnt sense. He told "whoppers" till no-one could believe his destination boards, and no passengers would travel in him.

He is a henhouse now, in a field beside the railway. If he still tells "whoppers" they can do no harm. The hens never listen to them anyway!